ESCAPE FROM...
Pompeii

by Ben Richmond
illustrated by Nigel Chilvers

little bee books

ESCAPE FROM...

Pompeii

This is a work of fiction. Any references to historical events, real people, or real places are used fictitiously. Other names, characters, places, and events are products of the author's imagination, and any resemblance to actual events or places or persons, living or dead, is entirely coincidental.

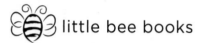 little bee books

New York, NY
Copyright © 2020 by Little Bee Books
All rights reserved, including the right of reproduction
in whole or in part in any form.
Printed in China RRD 1120
littlebeebooks.com

Library of Congress Cataloging-in-Publication Data
is available upon request.
ISBN 978-1-4998-1167-4 (hardcover)
First Edition 10 9 8 7 6 5 4 3 2 1
ISBN 978-1-4998-1107-0 (paperback)
First Edition 10 9 8 7 6 5 4 3 2 1

For information about special discounts on bulk purchases, please contact Little Bee Books at sales@littlebeebooks.com.

MARCH 20, 1759

The wind whips loose dirt from the workman's shovel and into his eyes. He tosses the scoop of soil to the side and wipes his face. It is hot here in southern Italy even in March, even between the glittering water of the bay and the looming mountain nearby.

"You know what I dislike about this job, Roberto?" he calls to the other, older workman who is with him.

"What do you dislike, Luca?" Roberto says with a smile, sticking his shovel into the ground. "Actually working?" He walks over to offer Luca a drink of water from his canteen.

Luca accepts it with a grin. "No, and it's not being

away from home, either." He points across the bay to Naples, the city where they both live. It shimmers in the light and heat.

Roberto takes the canteen back and drinks deeply. "What don't you like, then?" he asks and wipes his mouth.

Luca gestures to the work site. "This place is creepy."

The two are standing next to what had once been a house. Now, it looks like a hill with a house hidden within it. Walls are starting to take shape where the men have been digging. In the piles of dirt, they find bits of pottery and flakes of pale-colored paint.

"I don't like doing this. It's one thing to dig up a house, but I can't stand when we find . . . them," Luca says with a shudder, turning from Roberto.

Luca takes Roberto by the elbow and leads him to the edge of the lot. Across the flat plain, there are other groups of men like them. Standing together in small groups at work sites, they're surrounded by tools and tents and large piles of moved dirt. The top halves of buildings poke out of the ground where they have been working.

"The whole town was buried, Roberto! There's the gate through the city wall." Luca points down the hill. He then swings his finger toward a series of stone seats with tall grass growing between the aisles. "There's the amphitheater. And the street that led to it. It's just like our city!"

"It *is* just like our city, Luca!" Roberto says. His eyes widen with excitement and he gestures over the plain with both hands. "This is just what Naples used to be like. Our city is just a few miles away. Two proud Roman cities at the height of the Roman Empire. The only difference was Naples was farther away from the volcano when it erupted!" he said, pointing to the mountain in the distance.

Luca looks up at the sky. Roberto is always talking about Rome and its mighty empire, stretching from Spain all the way to the Caspian Sea.

"People walked these streets just as they walk

through Naples today, but here, nothing has changed! It's as if one day, a town was taken from the very first century and transported here to seventeen fifty-nine! We're the first to see its walls and streets in more than a thousand years!"

Luca meets Roberto's excited eyes. "Yes, I know. It's not finding the town that bothers me—it's finding the people who used to live here," he says.

Roberto looks worried. Luca seems on the verge of tears. "We keep finding bodies of people who were running away from the erupting volcano! I know you've seen them: people hunkered together, grabbing whatever they could hold! Men with money, or swords; children clutching their toys!" Luca sighs. "In the end, nothing kept them safe from Mount Vesuvius."

Roberto puts his hand on Luca's shoulder and leans in to meet his friend's gaze. "Luca, you are right. We must respect this place. But we must also learn from it." He clears his throat and raises his index finger. "'To be ignorant of what occurred before you were born is to always remain a child,'" he proclaims.

Luca smiles. "Who said that? That sounds familiar."

Roberto winks. "It was Cicero, one of those Romans I'm always talking about," Roberto says, gesturing to the buried structure they have been digging out. "This was his house."

Roberto's shovel suddenly flops to the side from its spot in the dirt pile. Clods of earth start tumbling down the mounds. All across the plain, workmen shout to each other and at the same moment, Luca and Roberto understand: It's an earthquake!

Then they hear it.

Part of Mount Vesuvius, the mountain that looms above them, is collapsing. The sound of stones slamming into each other cracks like a bomb going off. Thundering rumbles shake the ground. A *hiss*, like the sizzle of meat on a grill, increases until it becomes a roar. Parts of the mountain bulge and split open.

Roberto calls to the mountain, "Vesuvius! Be calm!"

Luca looks at his friend like he's crazy. "The mountain

can't hear you! Roberto—we need to go! I don't want someone else digging *us* up next!"

But thankfully, no one gets buried that day. The cinder cone on top of Mt. Vesuvius collapses, and the eruptions go on for ten days. Lava flows down the side of the mountain. The following year, 1760, a low part of the mountain cracks open. Lava flows across the farmland of Campania in what is today Italy. Mount Vesuvius will not stay calm. But these small eruptions are nothing compared to what happened over a thousand years earlier.

REALITY CHECK

WHAT IS A VOLCANO?

A volcano is an opening in the Earth's crust that allows lava, volcanic ash, and gas to come to the surface. Sometimes the lava is released slowly, and it cools to create a land mass, such as a mountain. Other times, the pressure builds up until it is released in a violent eruption that sends material high into the sky.

CHAPTER ONE

ONE THOUSAND, SIX HUNDRED AND EIGHTY YEARS EARLIER . . .

THALIA

Morning, the day before the eruption, August, 79 CE

As we walk from the docks, I look up the road. In the distance, I spot Pompeii. It's the busiest city I have ever seen—I mean, it's the busiest city that I'm seeing *again*. I have to remember that!

The traffic of the morning is all around us like a river that flows into the city gates. There are donkeys weighed down with heavy sacks and two-wheeled carts called *birota* that are pulled by mules. I even see covered wagons! They all slow down as they come to the walls of Pompeii. Mostly, it looks like merchants are bringing things to sell in the markets. Though maybe they are delivering goods to the big villas, the houses where the rich live. They bring olives and olive oil, big spools of wool, heaping sacks of lentils and walnuts and spices, jars of fish sauce, and freshly caught shrimp. Pompeii stretches up the hill toward distant mountains. Its rocky peaks glimmer in the early morning sunshine. The drivers call out to their donkeys and mules, and yell at each other. The air is full of the clanking of their bells, which I'm told is how they navigate Pompeii's narrow streets without crashing into one another. These are the very streets where I was born and where I met Lucius and Julia—

As I think all this, Lucius puts his hand on my shoulder and smiles. "Does it look like home, Thalia?" he asks me. Even though it's still cool in the early morning, Lucius is already sweating from carrying so much of our stuff. He lugs our gear in his *sarcina*, which is a group of bags tied together on poles. It's how the Roman soldiers carry their things.

"Lucius, you know I haven't been back to Pompeii

since I was a baby," I laugh, and he chuckles, too. He sets the sarcina down to wipe his brow and stroke his graying beard.

"Pompeii was a beautiful city back then," he says with a smile. "I can't believe I haven't been back in ten years!"

"Do you think it has changed much, Lucius?" I ask.

"I hope so!" Lucius says, making his face suddenly look serious and dramatic. He's an actor, so he's always doing things like this. It makes me laugh. "The last time I was here, they were still building the whole place all over again!"

"I thought you said that Pompeii was an old city—as old as Rome!"

"It *is* very old, Thalia. But cities are always building and rebuilding themselves. When you and I left Pompeii, they were rebuilding from a terrible earthquake!" Lucius's voice gets louder. "You see, five years before we left Pompeii, the god Vulcan was deep in his workshop in the earth making some new shoes for Jupiter. . . ."

"And five years from now, you'll still be telling that story and we'll *still* be waiting to get through the gates of Pompeii!" a woman's voice calls from a cart next to us. It's Julia! The third member of our acting troupe has arrived! Me, Julia, and Lucius. This morning, Julia's riding next to an angry-looking mule driver who seems mad that traffic has come to a stop.

While Lucius and I have to walk, Julia rides in a cart. Our musical instruments and theater costumes were just too heavy to carry from the docks all the way into the city. Besides, we need to be fresh for tonight's big show at some fancy local politician's house.

I like traveling and performing with Lucius and Julia, but they are a lot older than I am. My best friend is actually riding in Julia's lap, my little dog. Her name is Miya. At the sight of me and Lucius, I see Miya's head perk up and her stubby tail start to flit back and forth.

"We don't have five years, Julia!" Lucius calls back.

"We have so much to do! But first, we have to take the costumes to the laundry—they smell like the bottom of a ship!"

"Where is the house where we're performing?" I ask. "Can we see it from here?"

"No, the villa is through the city and beyond the northwest city gate. The driver has some deliveries to make on the way, but he and Julia will drop everything off when they're done. He said going through the city would be fastest way there, but . . ."

At this, the mule driver perks up. His bushy eyebrows raise high up as he looks angrily at Lucius. "You think the roads going to the other gate are free and open, actor?"

"Oh, don't listen to Lucius, my man," Julia says and pats the driver on his arm. An actor, too, she can really make a man feel like she's on his side. "Lucius is just angry because he's carrying a bunch of theater costumes that smell like rotten octopus."

The driver's one tough customer. Even with Julia's charm on display, he still goes back to glaring at the back of the cart in front of him.

"These costumes really do smell bad," Lucius says. "So let's drop off the laundry and get something to eat. . . ."

"And finally bathe!" Julia calls as the cart lurches forward with a start. Lucius pulls the poles back onto his shoulders and we begin to walk alongside a herd of goats. Just as the cart pulls forward, Miya jumps from Julia's lap and scuttles into the back of the cart. The driver yells, "Keep that dog out of there!" but Miya's already peeking out from the back of the wagon. She glances at me, at the goats, and then takes a deep whiff of the air. She must want to stretch her legs or chase the goats, because she leaps out of the back of the wagon and rushes toward us.

"Miya!" Lucius calls and Miya trots over, looking pleased.

"Did you miss me, pup?" I laugh.

Miya's attention is with us for only a moment before she catches the scent of sausage cooking somewhere inside the walls of Pompeii. She turns quickly, and it almost looks like her little legs are moving her toward the smell on their own. She starts to run off!

"Miya!" I yell, but I know there's no catching her. I look at Lucius, and his face says something like "I knew this was going to happen." Lucius seems to think Miya is more trouble than she's worth. And watching her streak away into Pompeii, a strange city we don't know, I think Lucius is probably right. But still, she's my dog.

"I'm sorry, but I have to go after her," I tell Lucius.

"I know," he says and laughs.

As I turn to see if I can squeeze through the crowd, I hear Lucius call to me, "Meet us outside the main baths after midday!"

"I will be there!" I call and realize that I don't have any idea where the public baths are in this town.

Lucius reads my mind. "Follow this road! The baths are on this side of the forum!"

"Thank you, Lucius!" I say. I wonder where the forum is. "I'll fetch Miya and bring her right back!"

"If you have a chance, see if you can find a better-behaved dog!"

I turn to Lucius, my eyes wide in mock horror. Even weighed down by the costumes, it's Lucius's turn to laugh at me being dramatic.

I'm an actor, too.

REALITY CHECK

What was the Roman Empire?

The Roman Empire was an ancient civilization centered in what is today known as Rome, Italy. It lasted from about 27 BCE until the 470s CE. At its height, it stretched from the Caspian Sea, near today's Iran, across northern Africa, and up into England. Across the empire, people could use Latin to speak to each other, in addition to whatever local languages they may have spoken. They followed Roman laws and used Roman coins to pay for things. Romans built roads to connect cities in their massive empire, and aqueducts to supply fresh, clean water. Even though it was long ago, people in ancient Rome had running water and were able to take warm baths. They were able to buy bread made from wheat grown in north Africa, eat grapes from Spain, and have cheese from Greece!

Pompeii was a Roman city in southern Italy. It was built across the bay from the city of Naples, which still stands today. People aren't sure how big Pompeii was in its heyday, but they think between 10,000–20,000 people lived there in the first century. Many Romans had summer homes in or near Pompeii.

CHAPTER TWO

FELIX

Midmorning the day before the eruption, AD 79

"Are you listening to me, Felix? You're hearing what I'm saying?" my teacher, a *litterator* named Stronius, yells right into my face.

I really should have run away faster, I think to myself. *What's he so mad at me for?* Stronius's face is turning red. *I just wrote on the wall. Everyone in Pompeii does a little graffiti every now and then.*

I give a quick glance around the circle at the other boys. They all look bored. Either staring out across the Forum or watching the litterator like he was a weird bird or something. I am one of the oldest students. We're all the sons of Pompeii's rich merchants and politicians. Thankfully, it's my last year getting yelled at by the litterator.

I'm just going to interrupt him, I decide.

"Yes, litterator," I say loudly and hope to stop his river of talk-talk-talking.

All day I put up with this: the litterator, my mother, my father. Everyone has something to lecture me about. It's like, they tell you to explore the truth, but you carve something true on the wall, and all of a sudden, you're in trouble for it!

The red-faced litterator seems to be wrapping up.

"Okay, I understand," I say.

"*What* do you understand, Felix?" Stronius growls slowly, angrily.

Time to take a guess. "I understand . . . that you don't think I should have carved 'Stronius knows nothing' into the wall?"

Startled pigeons fly off into the bright blue sky as Stronius shouts, "FELIX!" loud enough to be heard at the top of Mount Vesuvius. The other boys cackle with laughter.

"What?" I reply. "Are you saying I SHOULD have carved that into the wall?"

"You still don't know what this is about," Stronius says with a sigh.

I think it's unfair that he acts like being mad at me is such a burden for HIM.

"You just . . . don't . . . know," he repeats. "Your father may be one of the men in charge of this city, but that doesn't make *you* in charge. Someday I hope you realize that being a good man means serving . . . not being served."

I don't like him talking about my father and I wince at the mention of him.

But Stronius doesn't really seem mad anymore. If anything, he seems tired. It makes me feel a little guilty for what I wrote. I think about the poetry he tries to teach us. I pretend not to like it, but I do. I really like Virgil and especially Horace. In fact, Horace was the one who said, "What's wrong with someone laughing as they tell the truth?" Maybe Stronius isn't so bad after all.

"Everyone can go," Stronius says with a wave of his hands. "I'll see you tomorrow morning."

Everyone gets up, and as Stronius turns away, my friend Crispus walks up to me. He lives in a villa down the road from mine, just outside of Pompeii's city gates. We walk home together all the time.

"Can you believe Stronius?" I ask Crispus. He is a little smaller than me with curly light hair. My hair is curly, too, but dark. We walk together along the road that leads to the city gate. If you keep following that road, it takes you all the way to the next city, Herculaneum.

Crispus, who is always calmer than me, shrugs. "If you were a teacher, how would you like seeing graffiti on a wall that said you didn't know anything?" he asks.

"You know I don't want to be a teacher," I respond. But he does have a point.

"Well, I guess with Flaccus as your father, you won't be," Crispus says. "Flaccus is a politician, so you'll probably be a politician, too. Or a lawyer, right?"

I kick at a pebble that skips across the Forum, knocking up dust. "And have to go to more school? Stronius surely doesn't want that, and I don't, either."

We step between the big marble blocks that keep carts from going straight into the middle of the Forum. Before crossing the road to leave, I point up to the grand archway that spans over the road. My father told me it's a monument for some Roman general who fought a bunch of savages somewhere cold and far away. "Did that general guy go to school?"

"Germanicus?" Crispus asks, looking up. Ugh, *of course* Crispus knows his name. "Yeah, I think generals go to school. Though he was a soldier first."

"See? They're all gods and soldiers—none of the people who earn these statues sit around at school or talking to politicians."

"Felix," Crispus says, "there are a lot of statues of politicians. And every one of those statues and archways for gods or soldiers probably has a politician's name on

23

it. You know why? Politicians pay for things like this.

"Anyway," Crispus adds, almost like he doesn't want to admit it, "General Germanicus's son became the emperor, so even *he* was sort of a politician."

He's right, but I'm not in the mood for Crispus to be right. We walk through the city gates and out into the fields outside of Pompeii. The air is clear and a gentle, warm breeze blows by. Down the hill, we can see the vineyards where all of Pompeii's grapes are grown. I pick up a branch that's fallen by the side of the road.

"Maybe instead of a politician . . . I could be a gladiator," I joke, and swing the stick.

Crispus dodges the blow and laughs. "You better not hit me with—"

I strike his leg and he grabs another stick. We spend the rest of the walk home battling. When I reach the door to my house, Vitus, our porter, looks at me and laughs.

"Felix! You know your father is hosting a party

tonight, and you come home looking like you've been rolling in the dirt!" he says.

"Tonight?" I groan. "The usual crowd?"

Vitus shakes his head. "Oh, not just them. A senator is here from Rome for tomorrow's festival. We'll have music and food and clean, clean children!" Vitus says with a laugh. "Your father's orders."

I wave goodbye to Crispus, who starts up the hill toward his own home. The fun part of my day is over.

REALITY CHECK

WHAT WAS SCHOOL LIKE IN ANCIENT ROME?

Ancient Rome didn't really have "schools" like we think of them today. Only boys went to school and even then, only the very wealthy ones were allowed to go. Mostly, fathers educated their sons, but sometimes they would hire teachers who would instruct groups of boys. And they didn't have school buildings, so they would often learn outside, like in a square.

Ancient Rome was a long time ago, but even though things were different, they still had restaurants and churches, bakeries and banks, just like we have today.

CHAPTER THREE

THALIA

Midday, the day before the eruption

Pompeii is beautiful, but it's bringing me down. Or maybe it's just my endless search for Miya that's depressing me. I think I'll see her in the distance, but she's always gone by the time I get there.

First, I follow her up the road into Pompeii. Through the city gates are warehouses. Lots of the carts around me are just waiting to unload, so traffic slows to a stop. It lets up just in time for me to watch Miya dash around the corner up another street.

I run to catch up, but her trail leads me to a workshop that makes felt. Big spools of wool are piled up all over the floors and tables. The workers look at me uneasily, like I don't belong. Of course I don't belong here. I quickly glance around. My dog doesn't belong here either, but from the looks of it, she figured that out and is long gone.

"Did anyone see . . ." I project my voice across the workshop and everyone looks over at me like I'm crazy ". . . a little dog? My little dog? Miya?"

Everyone shakes their heads.

"Miya!" I give it one last call and run back out into the street. That was . . . embarrassing.

The streets of Pompeii are waking up, and the sun is getting higher in the sky. The streets are narrow passages with buildings that rise up sometimes four or five stories high. Workshops, storefronts, and restaurants, things like that, open out into the street. Behind closed gates, passages lead back to what look like gardens and what I eventually realize are the fancy homes of Pompeii's rich people.

Out on the street, merchants set up awnings above what they have to sell. I reach a corner and look around.

No sign of Miya. A man is picking up figs that have spilled everywhere and putting them back into his basket.

"Excuse me, sir. Have you seen a little dog?" I ask.

His eyes go wide. "With a little spot on its ear?!"

"Yes!" I shout! That's Miya!

"That little dog is a thief! It just helped itself to a mouthful of my figs and knocked the basket over when I yelled at it to stop!"

Hmm. That definitely sounds like Miya.

"Which way did she go, sir?" I ask.

"That way!" he points up the road. "But first, you have to pay for what your dog took!"

I love Miya, but I don't have any money with me. "Oh, you don't understand," I say, thinking quickly. "She's not *my* dog. She . . . stole some felt from me! I'm chasing her to get it back!"

"Why would a dog take felt?"

"To wipe her mouth after eating fruit?" I offer.

At this, both the fig merchant and I stop to consider how something that sounds almost believable is, in fact, just silly when you think about it for more than a minute. I take this moment to run in the direction he pointed.

Even though I was born in Pompeii, I haven't been back since I was small. Every turn is unfamiliar to me now. I start wondering if these windows where people buy food straight off the grill—sausages, fish, salted bread—are the same ones I passed already.

The temples though, I know I'm seeing them for the first time. There's a temple to Isis, who I think is a deity that comes from Egypt. But the winged man on the walls looks a lot like any Roman god, except for the wings, I guess.

The Temple of Jupiter looks a lot like the one we have for him in Sicily, except more people call him by his Greek name, Zeus, back home. Sitting on top of some huge stones, I see a fifteen-stair staircase leading up into the temple's entrance. Even with people up there burning meat as a sacrifice to the god, I don't think Miya's going to bother with these big stairs.

In the big, open square that is Pompeii's forum, men

in togas are standing around, looking important. Are they politicians, I wonder?

When the sun is nearing the highest point in the sky and the day turns hot, I head over to the baths off of the main road that cuts through town. They look nice. Everyone, rich and poor, goes to the baths, but it's pretty quiet here in the middle of the day. I spot Lucius and Julia waiting for me in some shade across the road.

They must see that Miya isn't with me, because the first thing Julia does is hug me. Lucius quietly offers me some bread and cheese. They must know I'm hungry, too.

"Any luck, Thalia?" Julia asks, and with my mouth full, I can only shake my head.

"I'm sure Miya will show up once she's done sightseeing," Lucius says kindly. Miya's still my best friend, but even if Lucius and Julia are older, I'm glad to have them.

We sit and eat and talk for a bit about what we can expect tonight—we are playing at the politician

Flaccus's house, which is located outside the northwest gate. Not the south gate we came in from the river, or the northern gate that leads to Vesuvius, but the one that leads to the neighboring city of Herculaneum.

Julia and Lucius are tired from traveling and decide to go to the baths. I wish I could go with them, but I have to skip the baths if I'm ever going to find Miya.

REALITY CHECK

WHAT ARE ROMAN BATHS?

Ancient Romans of all types used the public baths. It was a very popular activity that included hot baths, saunas for sweating, cold water, and space to exercise. You can almost think of it as a spa, shower, and gym all rolled into one. The baths were beautifully decorated—you can still see the ornate decorations on the domed roof of the central baths in Pompeii today.

CHAPTER FOUR

FELIX

Evening the day before the eruption

After I change into a clean tunic and wipe my face and arms with a wet rag, I wander out of my room and walk through the house. All around me, slaves and servants are setting lamps down and making sure they are full of oil. This is so the party can keep going on after the sun goes down. It shows politicians that you are happy to share your wealth with other rich people. I think about how the servants don't get to have any fun at parties like this and it sort of makes me mad.

Out by the front door, we have a bunch of benches around a courtyard that we call the "atrium." When people wait to talk to my father, this is where they sit.

And right now, even hours before the party, there's already a lot of old men waiting to talk to him.

I wonder if any of their news is actually important as I pass along the benches where they sit in their togas, fanning themselves and talking. They occasionally pop grapes into their mouths as servants rush to get them more water, more bread, more cheese.

"Of course Flaccus will want to pay to clean the statue outside of the baths," one man is saying to another. "And when he talks about it, he'll no doubt say that I, Gaius Pumidius Diphilus, gave him the idea!"

This is the life of a politician. Can you believe these people? All these men try to get my father to mention their name with his, or carve their names into statues with his—statues of other people! Statues of gods! And meanwhile, my father's job is simply to decide what things to put his own name on. I guess it's so that people will recognize him and someday let him put his name on even *bigger* things that get recognized by even *more* important people. But when I carve names on the wall, I get in trouble for it. What's the difference?

The middle of the atrium is open to the sky, and it contains a small pool in the middle. My father, Flaccus, meets with the visitors in a nearby room that's decorated with a lot of colors and paintings on the walls. I guess it reminds them that my father is very rich and important. That's also why he's throwing the party tonight. He wants to show off for the senator from Rome. Rome is the most important city, and so people from Rome are more important than people from Pompeii. Or so my father says.

I wander out to where the servants are getting ready to serve food for tonight and drink some water from the fountain. It tastes salty and bad. Normally, the water here tastes good. It comes directly from the mountains. This smells like rotten eggs.

Two strangers are off by themselves in a corner of the atrium. No one is talking to them and no servants offer them water or food, so they must not be important. And then I see—they're unpacking masks! They're actors, traveling entertainers for the party! Finally, people who don't care about being rich and powerful. I creep up quietly and listen to them.

"I'm sure she'll be here," the woman says to the old man. "Thalia is very dependable."

"I know she is, but she doesn't know Pompeii well," the old man replies. "She loves Miya and won't want to come here until she can find that dog!"

"So, she'll find the dog," the woman says, "and then she'll come. I know Thalia. She'll be here. Let's practice the music for tonight."

The two head over to the water organ on a nearby wall. It uses water to pump air through the pipes to make sound. My father is very proud of it, and he must have hired these travelers to use it to play music at the party. But the organ sounds a little weak, so I know something must be wrong with the water.

I think about how my father works so hard to make sure that I go to parties like this for the rest of my life. And then I look at Vitus and realize that *his* father probably worked very hard just to get him to be able to wait on these party guests hand and foot, and I feel sad.

REALITY CHECK

Slaves in Ancient Rome

Slavery in ancient Rome was different from slavery as it was practiced in the Americas in more modern times. It was still cruel and dehumanizing, but it wasn't based on race. Enslaved people could have been prisoners of war, captured foreign sailors, or even children that poor people sold into enslavement. They worked everywhere—doing construction, working in factories and private homes, and they blended in with the typical workforce. Some would be freed by their masters or could eventually buy their freedom. Romans accepted it as normal, but some, like the philosopher Seneca, argued that enslaved people should still be treated fairly.

CHAPTER FIVE

THALIA

Evening on the day before the eruption

I don't want to deal with this porter right now, but I have to because he won't let me in to the villa I'm standing outside of.

My feet are sore from wandering up and down the hills of Pompeii—this place was basically built on the side of a mountain! I'll admit I look a little dusty from the day. I mean, just this morning, I was a clean passenger on a boat, but then I wandered Pompeii's crowded, hot streets all day looking for Miya. I wish I had time for a bath. Still, this porter has to see things my way.

"Okay, look," I say, being reasonable, "how could I even know that there's an event going ON inside

41

Flaccus's house unless I was *supposed* to be there? I wouldn't, right? But here I am, telling you I am an expected guest!"

The porter gives me a half smile. "Girl, just because I know when the gladiator tournament is doesn't mean I'm about to grab a trident and hop into the arena." He bends over so he can look me in the eye. "We don't welcome beggars here, but we certainly aren't cruel either. I'll see about getting you something to eat, then will you kindly leave?"

"I'm NOT a beggar! I'm an actor!" I object.

The porter snorts, "Really? I wonder what the difference is."

Just then a slim, black-haired boy about my age pops his head around the corner. His dark eyes meet mine, and I want to take a step back. Who is this kid?

"You're not from around here, are you?" he asks, staring into my eyes.

"I was born in Pompeii actually," I say, "but now I live in Sicily."

The boy raises his eyebrows and looks at the porter. "You see? She's no beggar; she's a visitor from Greece!"

The porter sighs, but doesn't shoo the kid away. I start to put it together—*he talks to the porter like the porter is his servant. . . .*

"Please, kind stranger, come in," the boy says and gestures with his hand.

I look at the porter, who's now rolling his eyes and looking away like *it isn't my place to tell him what to do.*

I slip past the porter into the hallway. It smells like food, and the sound of laughter wafts over the quiet gurgling of the fountains. Lamps flicker in the evening's long shadows.

"Thank you. I just got here this morning, but my dog ran off and I've spent all day looking for her," I explain. I leave out just who I am until I can figure out who *he* is. We start walking toward the sounds of the party.

He puffs out his chest and plays the host, almost like Lucius would. "Think nothing of it! Dog or no dog, you can't miss this feast!"

I decide I like him. He's goofy, but he's helping me out. Maybe he's a servant in the house. Though he does seem awfully well dressed for a servant. . . .

"So, if you don't mind my asking," I mutter, trying to find the right words, "who are you?"

It sounds wrong, but the reaction's right. He laughs.

"My name is Felix, the son of Flaccus, the *duumvir* of Pompeii," he says.

I think to myself that I've never heard of a duumvir, but isn't this Flaccus's house? This must be his son!

Felix catches on and explains what a duumvir is. "My father's one of the top two politicians in the city. He's the one who put together the gladiator games and theater shows for tomorrow."

My blood runs cold. *Actors like me aren't supposed to talk to the family here.*

"And you are . . ." he says with that goofy, theatrical-host voice.

"Me? My name is Thalia and I'm . . ."

Just as the whole jig is about to be up, the lady of the

house runs out. "Felix!" she cries.

Like a swan, she fluffs over, her tunic trailing behind her. The air seems to fill with her perfume. "Felix—the water isn't working! The fountains are slowing to trickles, and none of the musicians can get any sound out of the water organ. I need you to find Gallus and have him fix it!"

"Oh, Thalia, you'll have to forgive me," Felix says. "This is my mother, Canace, and she has given me a very important job: finding our servant in charge of water, Gallus."

"Felix!" Canace cries. "Now!"

She half drags him out of the room and finally, it seems like I can breathe again.

"You actor girls should know better than to talk to rich politicians' sons," a voice says behind me, and I freeze up all over again. "Thalia, it's me!"

It's Julia. She scared me half to death.

"Come on!" she says as I cover my face in relief. "You're just in time!"

CHAPTER SIX

FELIX

I follow my mother through the house. She's managing to scold and yell at everyone we come across: The food is wrong, something is late, the decorations look off.

"And Gallus! Where's Gallus?!" she asks everyone. All of them have been working the party all day, so of course they don't know where our servant who specializes in water is.

". . . and the mussels were supposed to be warm, but they were served with all the cold shellfish—and I *saw* people notice. I *saw* it. That Hilaria raised her eyebrows . . . like her house is so much . . . Felix why are you walking so slowly?" she asks me, finally noticing me dragging my feet. "What is it?" she demands.

"I just don't understand why you care about all of . . . this!" I finally say.

"When you drink sulfur water for the first time, you will care, too, my son!" she says.

"Okay, not the water maybe, but," I search for the words, "do you care about impressing all of these people? Who cares what they think? Aren't we Flaccus's family? Isn't he in charge of Pompeii?"

"Felix, Pompeii isn't everything," she says. "Besides, you'll find in politics that you always need to remind people who you are and what you can do."

"Well, it must be a big blow to everyone here if the warm mussels got served with the cold shellfish," I joke. "But I don't see myself becoming a politician."

She ignores my quip, but she pays attention to the second part. She looks surprised, but then something in her seems to soften. She stops being a host, kneels down, and turns back into my mom.

"Felix, I know you don't want to do some of the things that you must," she says, "or that you'll have to go somewhere you don't want to, or turn into someone you don't want to be. . . ."

She struggles for the right words. "When I was much younger—older than you, but before I met your father—I was in love with a gladiator," she says, and laughs at the very idea. My jaw drops in surprise.

My mother also grew up in a good family. She was well taken care of. Gladiators, on the other hand, were slaves. Most of the time, they were soldiers who once belonged to an army that lost in battle to Rome. They would be taken captive and made to fight.

"How could you even meet a gladiator?" I ask.

"He used to come to your grandfather's house to deliver things," she says. "His name was Celedus and he was very large and handsome.

"One day before he was sent away after a delivery, the two of us and a few other servants had a chance to go for a walk," she goes on. "And that sounds very nice, but Celedus had us walk right up to the garum factory outside of town."

"The garum factory?" I ask.

"Yes, the garum factory, where they make fish sauce. We eat this sauce with almost all of our meals, and they make it right outside of town. Do you know how they make it, Felix?" she asks.

"No."

"They take raw fish guts, add salt and herbs, and just let it sit there in the sun," she says. "Now picture that. Imagine how that must smell."

"Why would you go to a garum factory and smell dead fish?" I ask.

"Celedus explained that life was like garum. You have to go through the bad parts to get to the good," she says.

"That's a pretty wise thing for a gladiator to say," I tell her.

"Well, maybe he didn't say that *exactly*," she says. "The truth is, he actually worked at the garum factory, but he got accused of stealing. And as punishment, they sent him off to be a gladiator.

"I was sad for him, but he told me something quite true," my mother says. "He told me it was better to work in a fish sauce factory than to be a gladiator and die for someone else's fun."

I think about this. I've never considered if gladiators ever wanted something . . . else.

"So," my mother says, rising and wiping her hands on her tunic, "we aren't making fish sauce and we aren't fighting in the amphitheater. But we are fighting our own battle here, only it's with water, right?"

I smile.

"Let's find Gallus," she says. "And that girl you were speaking to? She's more like Celedus the gladiator than she is to people like us. Leave her be."

I remember the wiry, mussed-up girl who I made the porter let in and it makes me smile. I wonder who she is?

I'll have to look for her when I get back from fixing the water.

REALITY CHECK

GLADIATORS!

Gladiators were, at first, criminals and enslaved people who fought each other—or sometimes even wild animals—for the entertainment of "civilized" Romans. Sometimes these events were held in big amphitheaters like the famous colosseum in Rome. By the end of the Roman Empire, though, about half of the gladiators were people who *chose* to fight for the money or fame it brought them. While in movies, it seems like gladiators always fought to the death, that wasn't the case. In fact, it would be very expensive to train a man who was only going to die right away, so gladiators would often be spared, especially if they had pleased the crowd with their bravery and fighting style. Still, the life of a gladiator was hard and violent, and meant being treated like a slave.

CHAPTER SEVEN

THALIA

In a corner of the atrium, I'm putting on a clean tunic as Julia brings me up to speed: Something has gone wrong with the villa's water organ.

"So right now, Lucius is out there reciting some poetry," Julia says, and we pause. Lucius's booming voice can barely be heard over the guests' chatting. "I don't think that's what they're in the mood for. They're talking all over him."

The day is starting to catch up with me—Miya missing, the streets of Pompeii, arguing with the porter, meeting Felix and definitely pretending to be his equal. Not *lying* to him exactly but . . .

"Thalia!" Julia says, and I snap back to the present and all of our problems right now: rude crowd, no organ, and how I'm going to be spotted the minute we start to perform and then thrown out for talking to Felix.

"You okay?" Julia asks. "Don't worry about Miya. She always turns up. She's tough and smart, just like you. After we leave here, we can look for her together."

"But first we have to play?" I ask.

Julia nods and picks up a tambourine. "I'm on tambourine, we'll give Lucius cymbals, and you'll have to play the *cithara*."

Lucius was a good organ player, but I'm very good at the cithara. It's a sort of harp set on top of a big box that makes its sound louder. I have been playing cithara since I was a little kid, and I still love it. The best cithara players from Sicily to Gaul are quite famous. Someday, that's going to be me.

"Um, Julia, there is one problem though," I start to say, when Lucius runs out to meet us in the atrium.

"Okay, that didn't go over great!" Lucius says. His

face is slick with sweat. "Are you ready to play?"

"Lucius, I need to—"

Lucius keeps talking. "These are some of Pompeii's richest and most powerful people, along with visitors from Rome! And of course, the water organ stops working tonight! The water stunk like sulfur before it went out. Do you have any idea how bad that smells?"

They both get like this with the rush of performing. Normally, I think it's funny, but right now I need them to tell me if I'm going to get in trouble for talking to Felix.

"Okay, we ready?" Julia asks, hitting her tambourine.

"No. There's a problem," I say. "Felix, son of—"

"Miya's still missing," Julia interrupts me.

"Hey, don't worry. We're going to find her," he says, "right after we play."

I look down at our bags that are piled around us. I get an idea and root around in one of them.

"We need to really give it our all out there," Lucius is saying. "Um, Thalia? Your cithara is already out; you were just holding it and tuning it."

Got it, I think as I pull out one of our theater masks. It's a big, goofy, smiling face of an old man. We use it for pantomime, so there isn't even a mouth hole on it, just holes for two eyes. No one will be able to recognize me. I slip it over my face, pick up my cithara, and in a muffled voice say, "This is going to put us over the top" like I'm completely sure of it.

I'm not sure, but here we go.

As we run back to the atrium after our performance, we're all laughing.

Wearing masks to perform music isn't very typical. It made us look like we were about to perform a play. I think Flaccus and his friends loved seeing something unusual. Or maybe it's just that I was playing the cithara better than ever. We came out in our masks, and a hush fell over the crowd. I started with a soft little melody line, rising up. Then, with a nod from me, Lucius and Julia came crashing in with the cymbals and tambourine! We were off like a runaway chariot!

"Flaccus looked delighted, didn't he?" asks Julia.

"When you've pleased the master of the house, what can go wrong?" Lucius responds.

I know how they feel—when a performance goes well, it feels like all the world is just like it should be.

REALITY CHECK

WHAT DID ROMANS DO FOR FUN?

Roman entertainment was pretty different from ours. In public, there were theater performances, pantomimed plays without words, and of course, gladiator fights. Sometimes, they fought against animals like bears or lions. Most often, they fought each other.

Roman homes usually did not have room to have people over for dinner, except for the very wealthy. Most people would eat at the small restaurants around town.

We don't know exactly what Roman music sounded like, but we know the instruments from artwork made at the time—cymbals, organs that were powered by the water flowing through the house, drums and harps, and lyres and citharas.

CHAPTER EIGHT

FELIX

Gallus is found at last, and after my mother yells at him about the water, he and I check the reservoir on the roof. Normally, it is full of water from the aqueduct and from rain. But it's August now, so there hasn't been much rain. It seems like whatever is wrong with the water flow in the house is wrong up here, too.

Gallus is a thoughtful guy who has been with us a long time. He knows everything about water and used to build aqueducts for the Empire. But even he seems surprised by the weak trickle we're getting—and he can't figure out what's wrong at our house.

"I think I need to see if the neighbors have this same problem," Gallus says thoughtfully.

I like the idea of visiting my friend Crispus.

"I'd better come with you, Gallus," I say seriously. "You don't want my mother accusing you of just going for a walk when we need you most."

Gallus looks at me and knows that I'm not very serious about this, but he sighs. "Alright, let's be off then."

We don't see Crispus, but we talk to his porter, who says they are having the same problem—the water is only coming out as a trickle and it smells like sulfur.

Gallus, who is always pretty reserved, seems worried by what we hear. He's walking quickly, and I want to walk slowly. It's a beautiful afternoon.

"What do you think this is all about, Gallus?" I ask.

He thinks for a moment. "Well, Felix, in the past," he says slowly, "all of these things—the slow water, the smell of the water—they meant something bad was about to happen. Before you were born, these same things occurred once before, and Pompeii got shaken pretty badly. There was a big earthquake that toppled buildings and cracked streets."

"So are we going to go back and warn everybody?" I ask.

Gallus's eyes go wide. "Who would listen?" he says, shaking his head, but then catches himself. "I could be wrong—I *hope* I'm wrong—but . . . wait!"

We stop and stand silent on the road. The wind ruffled the scrubby bushes and few tall trees around us. Dust whips into the air.

"Gallus?" I ask, not seeing what he's getting at. It's a calm, warm day.

"There are normally birds and insects out here," he responds.

Once he says that, I realize it is unusually quiet. "Maybe it's always still in the middle of the afternoon?" I offer.

Gallus groans. "So much trouble comes from not knowing how to listen," he says.

We get back to the house and Gallus goes to find servants to go with him into town. They will get water from Pompeii's fountains and haul it back.

I hear the sound of music from the other room and decide that watching a bunch of people struggle with water is even less fun than this party.

I scan the room. Old men are laying around, feasting. Earlier, everyone was talking, but right now they're all focused on . . . Thalia!

She's wearing a mask, but I know it's her. She's playing the cithara and playing it really well! The whole room seems hypnotized. It's pretty amazing. Gallus says no one listens anymore, but here are the most important people in Pompeii. And they're all silent!

Her fingers run up and down the strings as the other two musicians tap along, trying to keep up.

They finish, and Thalia rushes from the room as the others follow.

I have to meet them!

It takes me a minute to get across the room and get out to the atrium, but when I do, I nearly bump into Thalia.

"Oh, hello!" she says and smiles.

"Hey, that music—" I start to say.

"Wasn't it beautiful?" she says. "My family and I love to see music performed."

She's pretending that it wasn't her playing! I'll play along. "Your . . . Greek family?"

"Yes, my—they're all back, uh, inside," she says and points to the party.

While I'm deciding how much to continue with Thalia's lie, the older musician, the cymbal player, comes rambling over. "Thalia! We have to talk about our performance for tomorrow!"

Thalia tries to shush him, but he doesn't hear her. Instead, he notices me. "Oh, hello. You're the young master of the house, aren't you?" he asks with a dramatic bow. "You honor us with your presence!"

I bow back. "And *you* honor us with your playing. The cithara was especially skillful." Thalia's eyes get wide and she turns white.

"Come see us perform tomorrow at midday. It will be entirely different," the old man says.

"I'll be there," I say and look at Thalia with a smile. "My family and I."

REALITY CHECK

WATER IN ROME

An aqueduct is a channel built to bring fresh, clean water to towns and cities. Romans built huge, complex aqueducts that you can still see today in parts of Turkey, France, Spain, and Greece. The Romans relied on gravity to bring water flowing from lakes and rivers to fill fountains and public baths in the cities and also irrigate farmland to grow crops. It was a simple system, but it allowed Roman cities to grow bigger than the towns that just relied on wells or rivers. Some Roman cities had whole sewer systems. Water from the aqueduct would run in Pompeii's streets, washing away garbage and waste made by people and animals.

CHAPTER NINE

THALIA

I can barely focus as we pack up the instruments. I've been caught, but . . . maybe that's not a problem? Is that possible? I try to listen to Lucius, who is mapping out our plan for tomorrow.

"Our performance is at midday, so it's going to be hot," he says.

"I think we need to perform something dramatic— how about *Dykolos*?" Lucius says. "Julia, you'll play my daughter, and Thalia, you will play Sostratos, the son of a rich man. To win me over, Sostratos disguises himself as a poor farmworker who tends to my fields."

"Is this a part I can even play?" I ask.

"We don't have some young man hiding somewhere, so yes, with a mask, I think you can pull it off," Julia says dryly. "You are an actor, after all!"

I sigh. It's not a respected life I lead. Not like Felix's. "Yeah, I'm an actor," I agree.

All three of us look at the costumes, masks, and instruments all around us. "Let's leave this here," Lucius says. "We'll take only what we need. And we'll look for Miya on our way to my friend Celer's home. He's a baker and has plenty of room for us to stay the night."

With bags over our shoulders, we head to the door.

"Hey, Thalia!" Felix calls out. He's peeking out from behind a pillar, grinning. He seems like fun, and I'm sorry to leave. I never really get a chance to hang out with many kids my age. He's about to say something when his mom calls for him. She's really hollering. Felix rolls his eyes, waves goodbye, and disappears inside.

"Do you think you could get Felix to raise our pay, Thalia?" Julia asks, and Lucius laughs loudly.

They call me an empress the whole way back to the

gates of Pompeii. The roads are empty at this time in the evening. As we step through them, we pause to watch a pair of lamplighters. One holds the ladder as the other climbs up and lights an oil lamp that hangs off the wall. The sun is just now setting. Mount Vesuvius, which looms over Pompeii, is almost totally faded from view.

It's starting to get late, and I really miss Miya. I don't know what I'd do if I lost her for good.

"Okay, first thing we need to do," Lucius says and wipes sweat from his brow, "is drop everything at the baker's house, over by the forum."

As we walk through the city, Lucius and Julia seem worried about something.

"You know, the water smelled like sulfur before, but now it's totally stopped running altogether," Julia says, making Lucius frown.

"That's why we're getting this lovely aroma of Pompeii at night," he says, pinching his nose. When Lucius crosses the street, he carefully steps on the high stones like he's crossing a rushing creek. Builders put the stones in to keep people's feet out of the mud, vegetable scraps, and animal droppings that are all over the street.

"Is Pompeii always such a mess?" I ask.

"Normally, water runs down the streets and all of this," Julie gestures to the smelly trash in the street, "flows away."

We call out Miya's name as we walk. The shutters of nearly every building are closed, but sometimes, someone will open one and peep out to see who's yelling.

I feel like giving up for the night. After a whole day of searching, the stinking, dark streets of Pompeii don't seem like a fun place to be anymore. Just as we enter the forum, though, we suddenly hear a familiar barking. On her stubby legs, Miya comes up to us running! She doesn't look harmed in any way, but she sure seems mad to us!

"Hey, I looked for you all day," I say. "Don't you get mad at ME!"

"Something's got you really upset," Julia says to Miya. "What wrong, girl?"

Miya stops, her tooth snags on her upper lip, and she looks from my face, to Julia's to Lucius's.

Then we all hear it: a low rumbling sound, and seconds later, the whole forum, the whole town, starts to shake.

REALITY CHECK

HOW DO WE KNOW SO MUCH ABOUT POMPEII?

We know a lot about Pompeii for two reasons: 1. The Romans were great at keeping records, so in other places in their empire (and also found in the ruins of Pompeii itself) there are writings about Pompeii that survived the test of time. Its destruction was also witnessed by Pliny the Elder, who recorded the event and sent his account to his nephew before he died in the eruption. 2. The eruption covered and preserved Pompeii under volcanic stone and ash, ensuring that nothing changed for more than a thousand years. It was all just waiting for the city to be rediscovered.

CHAPTER TEN

FELIX

Later that night

As the party comes to an end, my mother doesn't seem relieved. She somehow seems even more stressed out about how it all went.

People have left and the sun is almost down. Servants light the lamps. Empty plates and cups litter our garden. The fountain in the middle of the garden bubbles weakly, and I think about Gallus.

"Were there enough roasted dormice?" my mother wonders out loud as she and I lay back on benches and pick at the food left on our plates. "Enough bread? Enough garum?"

"The servants are hauling away enough food to have a feast of their own. It's not like we ran out of anything," I say. I point to a group of politicians in their togas still laughing as they sit around. "If those guys wanted more, believe me, they would have taken it. I saw how much they stuffed into their mouths."

My mother tries to stop a laugh and snorts instead. She wipes a tear from the corner of her eye to keep it from messing up her makeup.

"We went to a politician's villa once that had oysters, and a boar was stuffed with wild thrushes, so when they cut into it, the birds flew off in every direction; you should have heard the people cry out!" she says.

"How did they get a boar to eat a bunch of birds?"

At this, my mother laughs out loud and I feel us both relax. The mention of birds reminds me though. . . .

"Mother, Gallus said something strange as we were coming back from checking on the water."

"Oh?" she says. "What did Gallus say?"

"He said that before the last big earthquake, things

like this happened—the water smelled like sulfur and the birds and insects went missing," I say.

"So, we don't have birds flying out from a boar, and that means an earthquake is coming?" she asks.

"No, not at the table, out in the fields!" I say. "There were no birds out in the fields."

"Why were you in the fields with Gallus?" she asks. I can see why Gallus didn't bring this up with her himself. She's really missing the point here.

"Never mind."

"Gallus used to work on the aqueduct. He's not a fortune-teller, okay?" she says. "I think it's time you got some sleep."

In my room, I pour myself some water and sit on the bench where I sleep. A servant has left a lamp burning. The light is almost all gone from the sky. I sip and look at the pitcher. The handle is shaped to look like a satyr— half man, half goat. It has horns, a pointy beard, and goat legs. He's leaning back against the pitcher to scratch his back, which makes the handle shape. With a beard and a smug look on his face, he looks just like the politicians who continue to lounge about in the other room.

Everyone listens to the old men, but they only care to listen to each other, I think. They don't listen to servants. Or their wives. Or me. The only thing they seemed to listen to was Thalia on the cithara.

I lie down and look up at the ceiling. The light flickers. The shadows jump. Suddenly, it feels like someone is dragging my bed across the floor! The house groans and I hear people start to shout. With a crash, the satyr pitcher falls to the floor. It shatters, sending pieces flying. I close my eyes and vow to always listen to Gallus and anyone else who knows exactly what they're talking about. Even if they're a servant, I don't care. I vow to do this if the house doesn't fall down on me!

REALITY CHECK

VOLCANOS AND EARTHQUAKES:
WERE THERE SIGNS THAT MOUNT VESUVIUS WAS GOING TO EXPLODE?
Volcanos will usually give signs that they are about to erupt, like tremors in the earth. Before Mount Vesuvius erupted in 79 CE, there were earthquakes. The water smelled like sulfur or "rotten eggs." In some places, the normal water supply stopped running completely. But there had been earthquakes in Pompeii before, like back in 62 CE. There are no recordings of Vesuvius erupting before then, however.

CHAPTER ELEVEN

THALIA

The night before the eruption

Everything that isn't held down, falls down.

The few donkeys and mules still pulling carts in the forum panic during the earthquake. Their owners are shouting in vain, trying to calm them down. It's not working. A wide-eyed donkey pulling a cart barrels past us, spilling lemons as it goes. Lucius grabs us both by the arm and we run to the center of the forum to avoid the flowerpots, windows, and shutters that are raining down and crashing around us. Big marble blocks keep the carts of panicked donkeys from dashing into the center of the Forum, so it seems like a pretty safe place to be. Miya tucks in by our legs as we huddle together.

The sound is so loud and strange that I'm not sure when all of the rumbling and shaking finally stops. Eventually, my courage comes back to me and I look up. The lamp that the lamplighters had just lit is swaying, casting dancing shadows as it rocks back and forth.

All around us, we hear the people of Pompeii calling to each other. They are cursing the earthquake, cursing Vulcan, the god who causes earthquakes in his underground workshop, calling out for their mothers, their husbands, their mules.

"What did Pompeii do that this keeps happening?!" a merchant shouts as he kicks at broken pottery and spilled wheat all over the street. He winces when his toe hits something solid in the center of the wheat—a dislodged street stone.

"You know, I think I remember now why I left Pompeii," Lucius says. "It always seems to be breaking apart." He stands and wipes the dust off his tunic's knees and his legs. Aside for feeling frightened, everyone seems okay.

Julia rises, shaking her head. "Then you shouldn't have moved to Sicily. Earthquakes happen there, too. Virgil wrote about it."

"I'll admit, I didn't study my Virgil before I left," Lucius says.

"Virgil's writing about the earthquake doesn't stop there—the mountain starts throwing fireballs, telling of Julius Caesar's death," Julia says, gathering up her bag. "Emperor Titus better keep a sharp watch in Rome. Flaccus, too. This is a bad omen."

"Julia, hush," Lucius says and looks at Thalia. "Are you alright?"

I wipe tears from my eyes that I don't remember crying. At any rate, I got my dog back. I'm done with Pompeii as soon as I can get out of here. "Can we go home?" I ask in a voice that sounds too small to be mine.

Lucius smiles kindly. "Tomorrow night, after we perform, Thalia," he says apologetically.

I know we can't leave before we perform in public tomorrow. Flaccus has not paid us yet for performing at his house.

"Besides, we've got Miya to keep us safe," he says, pointing to the dog that seems so frightened, she won't stop shaking. At the mention of her name, she looks at Lucius and I'm pretty sure she's thinking "Are you crazy, man?"

The lamplighters timidly set up their fallen ladder and go back to work, knowing that Pompeii will need light to clean itself up.

It's not supposed to be far to get to Lucius's friend's house, but because of all the confusion from the earthquake, it feels like the journey takes several hours. We finally round the corner and Lucius calls out that he sees it, Celer's door.

Lucius knocks and an angry-looking man swings open the door, holding a lamp. "Celer?" Lucius says.

"Lucius?!" Celer struggles to see through the dark of night by the lamplight and then seems totally confused until suddenly it all snaps into place: It's his old friend Lucius!

"Lucius! You've come back to town and you needed to shake all of Pompeii to tell us! Can't you do anything quietly?" Celer laughs. He looks about Lucius's age, but his hair has gone bright white. In fact, his whole outfit is all white, and when he hugs Lucius, *he* becomes all white, too. Then I realize Celer is completely covered in flour.

"Celer, you look too old to be up this late! And too old to be such a mess!" Lucius jokes. "Do you remember Julia?"

"Julia, yes! I could never forget her!" Lucius says, "But I'm surprised she's still dragging you around!"

"Well, she gets some help from Thalia here," Lucius says and brings me forward so Celer can see me.

"Is this . . . ?" He doesn't finish the question, but Lucius's nod says it all. "Why, it's Thalia! When you left

Pompeii, I was an old man and I'm an even older man now. But you were a baby, and now you're a young lady!"

"It's nice to meet you, Celer!" I say. "This is my dog, Miya." I point to Miya, who sniffs suspiciously at this flour-covered man's ankles.

"Well, come in, everybody. We've got lots of cleaning up to do, but at least the donkey is all calmed down now."

"You keep a donkey in your bakery?" I ask.

"He helps me grind the flour," Celer says, welcoming us in. "I hook him up to a mill that grounds the wheat, but tonight, the donkey decided that if the earthquake wasn't going to bring down the shelves where I store flour, he would do it himself, and so here we are."

In a stall in the back, the donkey's ears are flicking nervously. The big jar of flour he kicked over has spilled everywhere.

REALITY CHECK

WHAT DID ROMANS THINK CAUSED EARTHQUAKES?

Today, we know that earthquakes are caused by tension and pressure in the earth's crust, but ancient Romans didn't. They believed that when the gods defeated giants, they would put them into the ground and that earthquakes were the now-captive giants rumbling about. They also thought the god Vulcan working as a blacksmith in his underground workshop could cause them. Other Romans thought that there were chemical reactions happening underground and that these instances resulted in parts of the earth catching fire. It took until the nineteenth and twentieth centuries for people to understand what was actually happening.

CHAPTER TWELVE

FELIX

Back at Flaccus's house after the earthquake

It feels like the walls are still shaking, but maybe that's just servants running around. They are trying to put everything back in place, clean up, and bring more food and drink to the guests who are still here.

I walk out of my room and wander up the dark hall. No one's paying much attention to me. I can hear my mother shouting at the servants like this sudden disturbance is their fault. Or like someone is going to think it's *her* fault if she doesn't yell enough.

The porter brushes past me in a hurry. He only does this when there's someone important waiting to see Father. I sneak out to the atrium, and sure enough, a man is waiting there. He looks familiar, some city official who comes here a lot, I think.

The porter and my father come up the hallway and, I don't know why, but I duck out of the light and hide between some columns. I guess that this city official isn't very important because my father doesn't put on a show of how glad he is to see him.

"Flaccus," the man says respectfully.

"Let's talk in here," my father says gravely, and they both head to the door to his reception room.

It's so dark and the lamps don't do that much, so I run out into the garden and around the corner. Even in the dark, I can see the window to the reception room. Quietly as I can, I tiptoe over to the window to listen.

". . . water still isn't flowing into the cisterns, but they're both still three quarters full," the man is saying.

"What if we don't ration the water until *after* tomorrow's activities?" my father asks. "Do you really want a Roman senator to see Pompeii without her shimmering fountains? Do you understand how bad that looks?"

The man seems sorry. "But with the hot weather we've been having, if we let the stored water out all at once, there will be nothing left. Pompeii's supply will be emptied fast."

"Emptied?!" my father yells.

"Or we go back to a time when people get their water from the river. Like when we were just a small town," the man says quietly. "Water makes a city of thousands like Pompeii possible."

"Water *and* leadership," my father says, and they both sink into silence.

"Flaccus, the city just had an earthquake. So far, it doesn't look like any buildings have fallen. If the only thing we have to do now is save water, I think we're still in good shape," the man tries. "The senator will understand that. He'll praise you for making such a hard choice!"

"Yes . . ." Flaccus says. Even without seeing his face, I can tell he likes the idea. Of course he does, it makes him look great!

"Very well then, we'll save water," my father says, his mind made up. "Post signs that the fountains will only flow for two hours in the morning and two in the late afternoon. Then I want the town builders to fix the arches and check on the major buildings. I can't afford a repeat of that last earthquake—with piles of stones lying in every corner of the city for years. I was elected because I fixed the damage. For years, people said I rose to power from the rubble. I will not buried in it!"

"You are very wise, Flaccus," the official says.

"Send in my porter as you go," my father calls.

I hear the porter enter. "Quietly send the servants to get as much water as they can from Pompeii. There isn't enough for everyone. It's going to be a mess tomorrow morning," my father tells him. "We have to take as much as we can before other people find out."

My dad is going to steal water from Pompeii. I wish this was a surprise, but it's how my dad is. He cares more about himself than other people. From the sound of it, things are about to get a lot worse.

REALITY CHECK

WHAT KIND OF POLITICIANS DID THEY HAVE IN ANCIENT ROME AND POMPEII?

There were more than 2,500 posters for politicians found on the walls of Pompeii. It's not very different from the yard signs you can find in neighborhoods today before an election. In Pompeii, the top office was the duumvir. It was held by two men for a year at a time. They were elected by the men of Pompeii. Women were not allowed to vote or hold office, nor were the enslaved.

CHAPTER THIRTEEN

THALIA

Morning of the eruption

The next morning, we walk through the streets of Pompeii, and evidence of the earthquake is almost all cleaned up.

As we pass the fountain, though, it looks like water shortage is still an issue. Roman soldiers are standing around, telling people to stay calm. There is still two hours of water left, but people are crowded and acting a little crazy. Many of them look like servants that someone rich sent. They all seem to know that they can't go back empty-handed. One tall, thin man sets a full water pitcher on his hand cart and heads back into the crowd with an empty one. While he's gone, someone tries to fill their own vessel from the tall man's pitcher. The tall man sees the thief, runs over, and a shouting match begins.

As we get away from the fountain, the energy of the city changes. It has an oddly party-like feel. The festival is starting. The theater groups perform all morning in Pompeii's beautiful odeon, a big theater with rows and rows of seats. The seats are carved in a half circle—more than a thousand people can watch at once! I wonder how many are going to watch me when it is our turn?

Probably even more people will go to the amphitheater in the afternoon. That's where the gladiators are going to fight. First, they'll fight boars, then bulls and bears, and finally each other. Gladiator fights are competition for actors and plays, so we usually skip them. They are too scary for me, anyway.

We step around street sweepers. Everyone's missing the water this morning, but these guys might be missing it the most. Without water to wash all the trash away, they'll have to do a lot more sweeping. Julia talked about how in neighboring Herculaneum, they have sewers to take all this stuff away. But Pompeii is too old, so it has to rely on its gutters.

"The best we can hope for is rain," Julia says.

"After we perform, of course," Lucius corrects her, and she playfully rolls her eyes. We're all in a pretty good mood. It shouldn't be a surprise, but Celer had all the bread we could want for breakfast. There's nothing like a good night's sleep and a full belly.

The walls have notices painted on them, saying that Flaccus has brought the gladiator shows back to Pompeii and that theater performances would begin in the morning. They also say to vote for Flaccus!

At the theater, other groups of entertainers seem to be making Flaccus look pretty good. Jugglers clear the stage and a curtain is lowered for a pantomime show. Without saying a word, the actors perform a fun story of mistaken identity. From backstage, I peek out into the crowd. The seats aren't all filled, and people are sort of coming and going, but it seems like more and more people are there with each new play.

As the sun rises, slaves run fabric overhead, creating shade, and cooling the growing crowd. This makes everyone happy. Everyone except Lucius. "We're going to have to be even louder over the flapping of that fabric roof," he says. Julia and I share a look. Sometimes when Lucius is nervous, he gets like this—easily annoyed.

There's a big crowd now. Lucius recognizes a lot of people he hasn't seen in a while. Celer told us this morning that he would try to come, but he needed to get more water for his bakery first. He also needed to clean up some more.

I try to clear my mind of who else might be in the audience—senators from Rome, Flaccus, his wife, Felix. I think about what I know about Pompeii theater. The audiences here are supposed to be smart. Though I've heard they can also turn against a show they don't like quickly.

From behind the curtain, I hear crowds laugh at

some of the jugglers. It's time for us to get ready! I take my place, putting on my mask. Lucius starts things off and Julia is already onstage. I look to Miya, who's laying on the floor backstage. Actors from other troupes carefully step around her.

"Wish me luck, Miya!" I whisper.

Miya looks up, but she gives me that same weird look she had last night. The butterflies in my stomach turn to stone and drop. Something bad is about to—

CRASH! There's a deafening, smashing sound and another rumble. It sounds like thunder, but only if it boomed right outside your door and not up in the sky. I can hear the audience getting up and shouting. I rush to the stage to see them running out of the odeon and into the street.

I hurry to the backstage door. All the other actors are rushing out.

People in the streets either stand around stunned or are running. Everyone who is standing still is facing in the same direction. The look on their faces is a mix of horror and awe. Lucius and Julia join me, and we come around the corner to take it all in.

"Dear heavens . . . it's Vesuvius!" Lucius says. From the top of the mountain, a plume of smoke is rising and rising and rising. Even with everything around us shaking, it's the scariest thing I've ever seen. The sound of an explosion just keeps going, until it sounds like the mountain is roaring at us.

"Vesuvius is angry!" calls one man, as he runs past.

"We need to go," Lucius says in a low, but firm, voice.

A violent shockwave shakes the street and bricks fall from high points in the back of the theater. They break around us, and a big stone chunk crashes to the ground right in front of me and shatters in two. A rock flies right into Julia's ankle and she falls.

We run to her side. "How bad is it? Can you get down to the docks by yourself?" Lucius asks, and Julia yelps and shakes her head.

"Now we're leaving?" I ask. "What about the instruments? They're still at Flaccus's house!"

Lucius and Julia look at me. Lucius shakes his head. "And that's where they'll stay. Pompeii is in trouble and we've got to go right now. Look around!"

People are running, some even toward their homes that are closer to the mountain, but many more are just fleeing the city.

"If we get out, but we don't have what we need to live, then what?" I ask.

Lucius helps Julia up and she throws an arm around his neck.

"I'll meet you down at the docks! C'mon, Miya!" I say and turn to go.

"Hurry!" Julia yells after me.

I look to the towering cloud rising and spreading outward from Vesuvius. I start sprinting. I have to outrun the volcano.

REALITY CHECK

PLINEY'S EYEWITNESS ACCOUNT

We actually have an eyewitness account of the day Vesuvius erupted in 79 CE. The Roman official Pliny the elder was stationed on the Bay of Naples near Pompeii. In addition to being in charge of the Roman fleet, Pliny was a naturalist, which is an early sort of nature scientist. When Vesuvius went off, Pliny went toward the city to observe it, and also help a friend escape by boat. Unfortunately, Pliny the elder got too close and would eventually die near the volcano. His nephew, known as Pliny the younger, was also in the area and watched this all unfold. We still have letters from Pliny the younger to a friend where he tells the story of the eruption and his uncle's bravery.

CHAPTER FOURTEEN

FELIX

Morning of the eruption

The day begins with the usual boring social visit within Pompeii. I'm curious if anything big fell over in the night's earthquake, but it looks like things in the city are pretty normal.

We meet up with other rich families, and at one of the nice villas in town, I spy Crispus.

"Did you feel the earthquake last night?" I ask him.

"I did! It really caused a panic. My parents were scared, but nothing came down—just a few tiles off the wall," he says. "How's your house?"

"We were having a party, and it seems like everything was fine," I say. "Everyone was about to leave, but after the earthquake, they stayed and ate more. This morning, they were sleeping all over our garden."

Talking about the party reminds me. "We had great musicians, though—they're performing at the odeon in the middle of day," I say and look for my mother.

When I ask if we can go, she tells me no. "Theater is fine for some low people, Felix, but you need to spend more time around *our* people," she says.

"Our people" seem to spend all their time talking about the price of fish and the water supply, or what's going on in Rome or other places far, far away. I am so bored. Crispus and his family leave and I find a nice spot in a garden to sit. I hope something exciting happens today.

Finally, my mother tells me we are heading to the amphitheater to meet up with my father. I don't think either of my parents really like the gladiator matches, but all over the city, my father has paid people to paint advertisements for today's tournament. All of the posters say "Brought to Pompeii by Flaccus." Because of that, he needs to be there to start the tournament off with a big speech.

Our servants are waiting by the door. I haven't had a chance to tell Gallus that he was right about the earthquake. But as I'm walking over, we all learn just how right Gallus was.

It sounds like the wheels of a hundred chariots on the road. It sounds like stone falling onto stone. It sounds like the roar of lions or the roar of a crowd, or maybe that's just the sound of everyone starting to scream all at once.

I turn around and see that Mount Vesuvius, which looms over the city, is on . . . fire?! Or at least something inside of it is. Smoke is rising from the top of it, higher and higher, like a pine tree made of ash! The sound gets louder and the earth starts to shake again, more violently this time.

I turn, and Gallus is next to me, looking up at the mountain and the column of smoke that keeps rising. The sound is getting louder.

"I thought last night would be the worst of it," I tell him.

"I think tonight's going to be worse," he says. "We should hurry."

Gallus has been right this whole time, and I remember my vow to listen to him. My mother seems shocked, staring up at Vesuvius. The ground shakes, but she's totally focused on the mountain.

My father talks a lot about leadership, and even if I don't want to be him when I grow up, I do want to listen to people who know what they're talking about, and I'd like to help lead those who don't. So I touch my mother on the shoulder. She looks at me, but doesn't really seem to see me, or how bad things have gotten.

"Mother? Mother, we have to go!" I say. "We can't stay here. Let's go now."

"Go?" she says like she's waking up from a nap.

"We need to go home," I say and help her up.

Out on the streets of Pompeii, some people are running and shouting, and others are seeking safety indoors. Normally, citizens do a pretty good job of getting out of the way of people like my mother and I, or else our servants brush them aside if they won't move. But it seems like with everyone's eyes firmly planted on Vesuvius, no one notices our fancy clothing or my mother's makeup.

Smoke and ash start to fall down on the city, looking at first like fog, but smelling like burning sulfur.

Then it starts to rain stone. It sounds just like rain at first, then maybe hail. Small bits of light rock start falling, not any bigger than a pea. Still, they're rough and hot, and they sting when they hit my face.

Shielding his eyes, Gallus leads us under the high roof of the temple of Isis, where others have already gathered to get away from Vesuvius's wrath and anger.

I pick up one of the larger bits of stone that has fallen, and it's light and full of holes—not like cheese, more like a piece of bread. I guess that's why they're being thrown through the air. I look at our group. We're covered in ash just like everyone else. My mother doesn't look any richer than Gallus anymore, but she does look much more scared than him.

"We should keep moving," Gallus says.

"Can't we wait inside until the stones stop falling, at least?" I ask.

"That's only pumice, and it's just starting," he says.

"Then we need something to shield my mother with," I say, "or else she's not going to make it. Maybe you two can hold some fabric or something over her," I suggest to two of my mother's servants, who look at me like I'm crazy. They turn to Gallus and tell him that they're leaving.

As they head out, another person and a dog come into the shelter of the temple's tall ceiling. They're so blanketed in ash, I don't realize it's Thalia until she looks right at me and says, "Felix?"

"Thalia! What are *you* doing here?" I shout. I can't believe she's here!

"I'm going back to your house for our instruments, and then we're getting out of Pompeii. Lucius says this is bad," she says. "But now, I don't even know if it's worth trying to get our stuff."

"This *is* bad," Gallus says.

"Here, we can help you! We can go together," I say. "If we need to leave, my father can get us passage on a boat!"

Gallus and Thalia look at me with tired eyes, but they both know that if anyone is going to get through this, it's a rich man like Flaccus of Pompeii.

REALITY CHECK

WHAT HAPPENED WHEN VESUVIUS EXPLODED?

The eruption started in the early afternoon, and pumice began to fall on the city. Judging from how large the town was, and how many bodies were later uncovered, it seems like the population had a few hours to escape the worst of it. Some volcanos spew lava, which are rocks that are so hot, they're nearly liquid, but with the eruption in 79 AD, Vesuvius's explosions primarily were made of hot ash, pumice, and scorching, poisonous gases.

CHAPTER FIFTEEN

THALIA

With Felix and his mother, Gallus and Miya, we can only move slowly through Pompeii. There is still half a city to cross and the streets are getting clogged with overturned and abandoned carts. Animals—donkeys, mules, and horses—are now running loose, panicked. Merchant stalls have been thrown over or have collapsed under the weight of the falling pumice piled on top of them.

And the pumice just keeps building up! It's up to our ankles on the ground now. It's rough and hot and stinging. I pick up Miya—I don't think she can run through this anymore.

Vesuvius doesn't seem to be stopping. The ground is

still shaking and groaning, and ash is everywhere now like a thick fog. It's hard to breathe and even harder to see. It looks like the sun is going down even though I know it's only early in the afternoon.

"When we get to the forum, we can cut right across to the left," Felix shouts.

"I know that seems faster, but we should stay by the walls," I say. "They'll shield us from falling debris as much as anything can."

Canace coughs. "And what if the walls fall?" she asks.

I think. "I guess . . . then we're trapped anyway. But that's a good thing to watch out for!"

Felix laughs and I guess it does sound a little funny, even if Canace doesn't seem to think so.

I don't even recognize the forum when we get to it, so it's good to have Felix with us. Just last night, even after the first earthquake, this was the heart of Pompeii, and look at it now. . . . You can barely see across it. The glass windows of the nicer homes that line the square are all broken, and I think about how expensive it will be to replace them. Then I catch myself wondering if there will be anything left to replace?

We follow in a line along the walls, when suddenly a man kicks open a door from the inside, and carries a woman out. Even though everything smells like ash, the air here smells like a different type of burning—their house is on fire! They're so covered in soot that it takes a second to realize the woman is holding a small child. Tears roll down his face, leaving trails in the soot, as all three of them cough and gasp in the blackening air.

As we reach the corner of the forum that leads to Felix's house, the earth groans again. Chunks of the great archway in the corner start to fall around us, and I grab Felix by the wrist. Gallus does the same for Canace, and the four us barrel forward, the sounds of huge bricks falling behind us.

Moving is hard and only getting harder.

"The gods are punishing us!" I hear a woman cry.

"Pompeii is ruined!" a man yells.

The crowd grows thick near the city gates with

people hauling whatever they could grab on their way out of town. People drag their curtains, or food or chests full of . . . money, I guess. Felix and I try to stay together and keep each other upright. Then we hear his mom scream as she falls. People start to lurch over her, and she can't get up. She's being stepped on by the crowd!

Like a hero, Gallus shoves his way through the masses and grabs her by the shoulders. He lifts her off the ground and sets her on her feet. She coughs and shakes with fear. But we have no time to wait. Gallus grabs her hand and pulls her along behind him.

Regrouping outside the city walls, we're all covered in scratches and bleeding from cuts. Canace's dress is stained and she looks like a completely different person. The rich wife is gone. She's now just another scared person running for her life.

The fields outside of Pompeii are already covered in an unmelting snow of ash. Wind kicks up cinders that sting my eyes.

It's quieter out here, but I can still hear the fires

crackling through Pompeii behind us in between Vesuvius's roars.

I want to rush ahead, but Felix has to go slowly to encourage his mom along.

"We're out of the city now, but we have to keep moving!" he says.

I wonder if the porter's even going to recognize us, but when we get to the door to Flaccus's house, he's nowhere to be found.

Once inside the doorway in the covered area within the atrium, Canace finds a bench and sinks down onto it with a sob. Felix sits next to her and puts an arm around her.

I peer across the open-roofed atrium, now covered in pumice. Our instruments are still sitting in the corner. A few servants are running around, but I guess this is as good a time as any to grab our things.

As I run over to them, I hear someone call out, "Stop! Looter!"

"I'm not a thief. These are mine!" I stammer, but the

man comes right up to me and grabs me by the arm.

"Hey, leave her alone!" Felix shouts, standing up and running toward us.

The guard raises his hand to strike Felix when Canace shouts, "Vitus! It's us!" All of a sudden, the guard recognizes Canace and Felix. He looks scared. He was about to strike Flaccus's son! He drops my arm.

"Canace, forgive me! We've been looking everywhere for you and Felix!" he says. "You have to try to get Flaccus to leave! He won't listen to us!"

We look at the cracking walls. It seems impossible that we were all here for a party just last night.

"We can all leave together by boat! We can take it on the river and then out to the bay!" Felix says.

"No, we won't, Felix" a deep voice says. It's Flaccus. He isn't covered in ash; he's standing tall and angry, like if he could find the god Vulcan, he would command him to stop, and the god would put his hammer down. But Vulcan's not nearby. Only Felix and Canace are. So, he orders them, instead.

"I'm the duumvir of Pompeii, Felix," Flaccus says. "We must stay with our city in its hour of need."

I'm not sure how to argue with someone like this.

"A mountain is coming down upon us, Flaccus," Canace says, the first to find her voice. "What good is staying here going to do?"

"We won't be seen running in fear!" Flaccus shouts.

"It's not fear! It's just being smart!" Felix bursts out.

I double-check our bags—the instruments are there, as well as the theater gear we no longer need for today's now-cancelled performance. I have a plan.

REALITY CHECK

DID LAVA BURY POMPEII?

In movies, the big problem with volcanoes is hot lava, flowing out and turning the world to fire and stone. But the danger with Vesuvius was not only the hot stones and ash that it ejected, but also the hot, unbreathable gas that escaped from it. Later eruptions from Vesuvius would have more lava.

CHAPTER SIXTEEN

FELIX

No one is listening to me. Maybe someday they will when I'm an old man, but right now, it doesn't feel like I'm going to get that chance.

The porter helps my mother to sit down in the area where we were hosting a party last night, and my father goes to his reception room. Gallus quietly heads to the doorway. It looks like he's leaving for good. Before he steps out, he gives me a deep nod. Somehow it makes me feel brave.

Thalia looks at me. "If you want to go with us, we can go," she says.

"They won't listen," I say.

"Julia and Lucius are waiting for us at the docks. We can go to them now," Thalia says. "Look, I know this is your family, but . . . Lucius and Julia took me in. They became my family. They would do the same for you."

I think about it. Earlier today, everyone knew my future was to be a politician, probably in Pompeii, like my father. Today, I might be throwing that all away. I don't know if Pompeii has a future anymore, or if my father does . . . but I guess I can give one to myself.

"Let me talk to my mother—maybe she'll listen," I say. We walk over to where she is laying down. The plates from last night's feast are all gone, and it's messier than ever. The middle of our courtyard is slowly filling with ash and pumice, like it is everywhere else. They say the rain falls on rich and poor alike.

"I don't think Pompeii will survive this," I say to her quietly.

She doesn't look over at me. "You're right," she whispers, eyes closed as she rubs her temples. Finally, she looks up and meets me eyes. "I'm sorry."

"I love you," I say. "Thalia has a plan for us to escape. Come with us!"

Tears well up in her eyes. "I love you, too," she says. "But there's no way your father will let us leave. How would we get out?"

Thalia says, "We can act!" and holds up three theater masks.

It's not like anyone can recognize my ashen clothes, but now with an old man mask on, no one bothers to even look at my face. For the last time, I walk past Vitus, the porter, and back outside into Vesuvius's eruption.

Once outside the walls of my home, I take the theater mask off. Maybe it helps block falling pumice, but I'm already having a hard-enough time seeing the darkening sky. Thalia does the same, and so does my mother. We're lucky that Thalia's troupe has three actors. I don't know how we would have gotten out without these masks. It was strange to see my mother playing along. She's been so proper my whole life. Everything has changed now.

Without the masks on, it's easier to spot the larger, flaming stones that the volcano is throwing. Rocks the size of melons make long, colorful arcs as they crash down around us.

Before we start back to Pompeii, I look around. It seems like as much smoke is coming from the city as is from the mountaintop, but it's hard to say. Everything everywhere is on fire.

"I don't think we should go back into Pompeii," Thalia says.

"But that's the most direct way to the docks," I say.

"I know, but it was bad before down there, and it's getting worse," Thalia says. "Do you know another way?"

I remind myself I need to listen if I'm going to help. Thalia is right.

"We can stay outside the city walls and go through the fields," I say, pointing in that direction. Thalia picks up Miya and says something kind to the whining dog, and we start toward the outer walls of Pompeii. Mother is carrying some instruments, and I have everything else.

The sky has turned a bloody red. Sudden flashes light our way, followed by a rumble that sounds familiar—lightning and thunder are crashing around above Vesuvius.

"Now, Jupiter has joined Vulcan in ruining Pompeii?" I joke, and Thalia nods that she gets it. I just want to keep talking, about anything. Stone and ash covers everything as far as I can see. It's gotten hotter than any summer day. I'm sweating and it's hard to breathe.

"This is all vineyards," I say, like I'm giving them a tour. And maybe it is: the last tour of Pompeii. "I mean, it *used* to be vineyards." The plants are covered in ash, and the trellises that the vines ran on are falling over.

"I don't think this is going to be a good year for wine," Thalia jokes back, and I give her a nod that says I get it.

We reach the walls and get a little bit of shelter from falling ash and stone.

"It smells like wood is burning," Mother says.

"I think that's the city," Thalia says, and she's right. The sound of the volcano roaring, of floors falling down in burning buildings, it's all just one giant noise now. We pass another gate to Pompeii and a few people are running, carrying what they can. Now everyone in Pompeii, it seems, has gathered on the docks.

REALITY CHECK

FIRE IN THE CITY!

Fires were a real problem in ancient Roman cities. In 64 CE, a fire started in the city of Rome and lasted for almost a week. Although what you can see of ancient Rome today is made of stone, those are the only portions that have survived all these years. The ancient city itself was made of wood, and lit with candles, fires, and oil-burning lamps. Fires were a huge, and common, problem.

CHAPTER SEVENTEEN

THALIA

I set Miya down before we head into the crowd on the docks. Boats of all sizes and designed for all purposes— some for shipping goods, some for cruises, some that ferry people from Pompeii to Naples—are all leaving. They're weighed down, full of people, and overflowing with everyone's belongings. Still more people are waiting on the docks, arguing with ship owners. I don't see Julia or Lucius anywhere.

I start to wonder if maybe we're too late, if Julia and Lucius would have just left without us. How could you blame them—they didn't know when or if we'd be back.

Felix and I keep looking at each other. I think he's thinking the same thing I am, that we're on our own.

I hear a dog bark—is it Miya?

"Miya!" Felix calls out before I can.

Miya is moving through the crowd. We follow her barking and push our way forward. The docks are hazy, the winds coming down from Vesuvius keep getting heavier, and the sky darker.

In the light of a flash of lightning, I think I spot Lucius. He's as covered in soot and ash as everyone else, but I think I can make out his beard and his big eyebrows

"Lucius!" I yell, but the thunder and rumbling drowns me out.

The crush of people sways me back and forth, and I lose sight of the man I think is Lucius. Waves of hot air seem to roll through the crowd. I'm hot. I'm exhausted. I think I'm going to faint if we don't find them soon.

"Thalia! There he is!" Felix shakes my shoulder.

I want to cry. I want to sit down. But before I can do

anything, I hear the clear, loud voice that Lucius uses onstage say, "Let them through!"

He wraps me in a hug right there in the middle of the crowd. Then he grabs the heavy bags and instruments and leads us down to the same low, flat boat we arrived on. Somehow, Lucius and Julia were able to get all of us aboard the ship. Miya, suddenly brave, runs ahead and scampers across the gangway right onto the boat. It is tossing up and down in the choppy water. I, then Felix, then Lucius, run after her and climb down to its deck.

On board the boat, people are sweeping and shoveling pumice into the water. I look for Miya and see she's found Julia. Julia pats the dog and looks to us with a smile. "Felix, are you joining on us for our pleasure cruise?" Something about her calmness makes us all laugh. Then she sees Felix's mother.

"Julia, this is Canace, Felix's mother," I say, introducing them. Canace's clothes are dirty and torn.

She looks tired and scraped up from our escape. We're all equal here.

"I guess we're the hosts now," Julia says. "Well, welcome aboard."

"Where are we going, Julia?" I ask.

"First, this boat will take us to Misenum, and if we need to, even farther," she says calmly, and I immediately start feeling better.

The boat lurches out from the dock as we push off. It's crowded with other people who are also fleeing Pompeii. They hold their children, their jewelry, whatever they could grab, and they sway with the movement of the boat.

"I think the air is making me feel sick, Lucius," I say. "Can we go below deck?"

"If we have to, Thalia," he says and smiles. "I'm sorry to say the air down there is almost as bad. This boat is normally used to ship out garum."

In the lightning flashes coming from the top of the mountain and the fires burning, we catch glimpses of

Pompeii. The city looks mostly empty. A wave of hot air ripples through the boat.

No one is going to see Pompeii for a long time.

REALITY CHECK

HOW LONG DID THE ERUPTION LAST?

Vesuvius continued erupting all night and into the next day. But by that first nightfall, a volcanic column of hot air and ash above the mountain collapsed and fell down over the region. Hot, volcanic debris and poisonous air in what scientists now call a "pyroclastic surge" swooped down from the mountain. Those who didn't leave Pompeii were hunkered either indoors or under two meters of ash and pumice that thickly covered everything. The temperature seems to have reached 572 degrees Fahrenheit, but too quickly for anyone there to know what was happening. Pompeii and those left behind would be buried under three meters of debris.

CHAPTER EIGHTEEN

FELIX

A year later

I haven't gone back to Pompeii. I hear it's buried. Some people have dug into the rubble, looking for money or riches, but that sounds ugly to me. I've also heard that the whole coastline has moved out, that you can't even reach Pompeii by boat if you wanted to, even if it were still there.

We took the garum boat to Misenum across the bay, and then kept going on until we reached Naples. The town was full of Pompeii refugees, and anyone else who escaped the area. I didn't find my father, or anyone else I knew among them. I think about Gallus. I wonder where he is now. Without him, we wouldn't have made it.

Instead of becoming a politician, I'm becoming an actor, which is a surprise. I can play a young man better than anyone else in the troupe, and with a mask, I can play an old man, as well. Mother is adjusting to our new life, too. As she says, "Putting on a play is almost the same as putting on a good party. Everything has to be in the right place, and everyone needs to know their role." It's shocking, but she's right.

Our newest play is the story of a young actress from a faraway land and a distracted schoolboy. They meet and see a beautiful city's final days. It's a story of bravery and tough choices in the face of danger. And the best part about it is that they make it out alive.

REALITY CHECK

Is Mount Vesuvius going to erupt again?

We don't have any records of the eruptions of Mount Vesuvius before the one that erased Pompeii in 79 AD, but we have accounts of the many eruptions that happened afterward. An especially large eruption in 1631 buried what was once Pompeii and many other nearby towns in lava.

Vesuvius hasn't erupted since 1944, which is unusual for it. Three million people live close enough to be affected by an eruption, and 600,000 live in what's referred to as its "danger zone." Scientists and politicians are constantly working to improve plans to evacuate those 600,000 people if they have to. It would take about a week, and the plans all give two or three weeks' notice before the eruption. Vesuvius is closely watched, and we know what warning signs to look for, but officials worry about sending out a false alarm, or letting people know too late. Like the time of Pliny the Elder, the mountain is still very much alive.

62 A.D.—Near Pompeii and Herculaneum, an earthquake occurs, resulting in severe damage. It was most likely caused by magma, underground, liquefied rock, rising to the surface.

August 79 A.D.—Tremors are felt in the area as magma forces its way through Mount Vesuvius.

August 24, 79 A.D.—Around 1:00 p.m., Vesuvius erupts. For the next 18 hours or so, pumice and ash shoot out from the volcano and rain down. The eruption clouds the sky and brings on near-total darkness. Temperatures rise to nearly 570 degrees Fahrenheit.

August 25, 79 A.D.—The ash cloud clears up, but Pompeii has been completely covered in nearly 10 feet of pumice and ash. It is estimated that the eruption killed 2,000 people in Pompeii and 14,000 in other towns and cities nearby.

1748—Pompeii is rediscovered by a surveying engineer. Archaeologists have been working on uncovering all of Pompeii ever since. It is slow work because the ruins are very fragile. Scientists believe that some of the city needs to remain underground to preserve it.

FIND OUT MORE

Kunhardt, Edith. *Pompeii . . . Buried Alive!* New York City: Random House Books for Young Readers, 1987.

National Geographic Kids' Pompeii Page: https://kids.nationalgeographic.com/explore/history/pompeii/

O'Connor, Jim. *What Was Pompeii?* New York City: Penguin Workshop, 2014.

Waxman, Laura Hamilton. *Mysteries of Pompeii*. Minneapolis: Lerner Publications, 2017.

SELECTED BIBLIOGRAPHY

Beard, Mary. *The Fires of Vesuvius: Pompeii Lost and Found*. Cambridge: Belknap Press, 2008.

Berry, Joanne. *The Complete Pompeii*. England: London: Thames & Hudson, 2007.

Harris, Robert. *Pompeii*. New York City: Paw Prints, 2008.